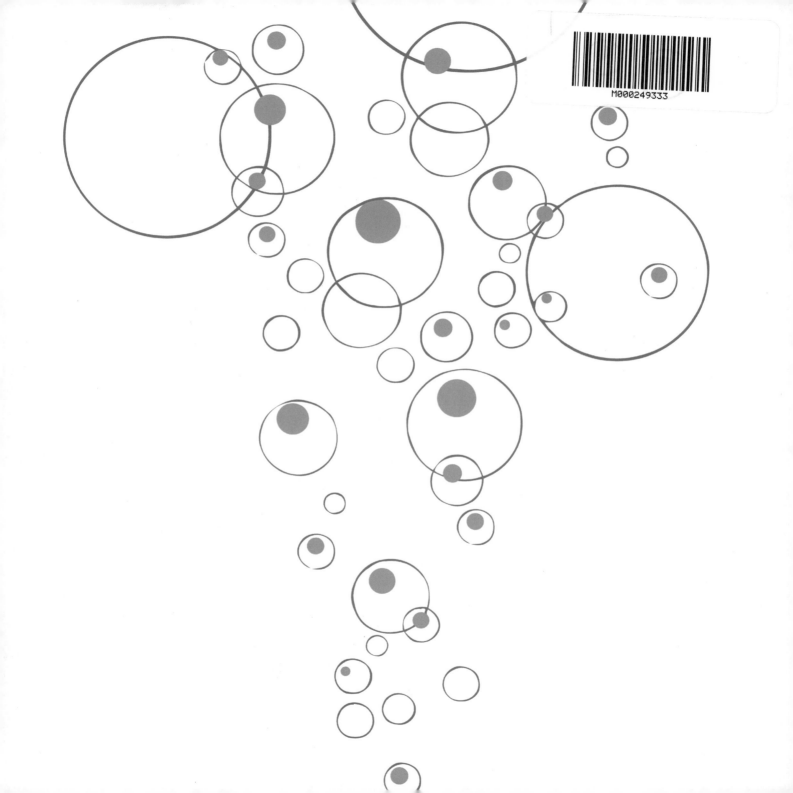

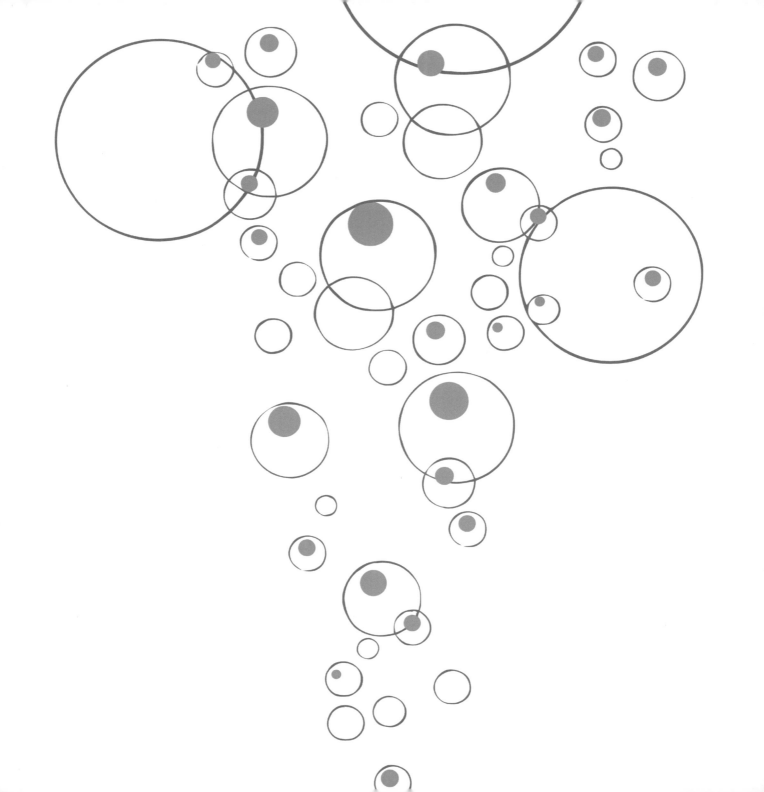

a patchwork fish tale

30th Anniversary Edition

by

Published by Stewart Moskowitz Media
ISBN: 978-0985146733
Original edition published in 1982 by Simon & Schuster, New York

Once there was an aquarium.

In it lived some rabbit fish, some duck fish...

...chicken fish, hippo fish, and a fat cat fish too.

There were tiger fish and flute fish...

...and then there was the biggest fish of all,
the patchwork tooth fish.

One day, the patchwork tooth fish was hungrier
than usual. He swam around and thought the duck fish
would be mighty tasty, so he sneaked up behind them...

...and before the duck fish knew that he was there,
he swallowed them up in one big gulp!

The patchwork tooth fish grew a little bigger,
and he now had a new duck patch.

But the duck fish did little to satisfy his appetite,
so he looked around and spotted the rabbit fish.

He swam up behind them, opened his toothy mouth,
and in one gulp swallowed the whole school!

He grew even bigger!
And some more
patches appeared.

I'm getting to be
one heck of a fish.
Bigger and brighter
and better than ever,
he thought.

But the patchwork
tooth fish was *still*
hungry.
So he looked
around again.

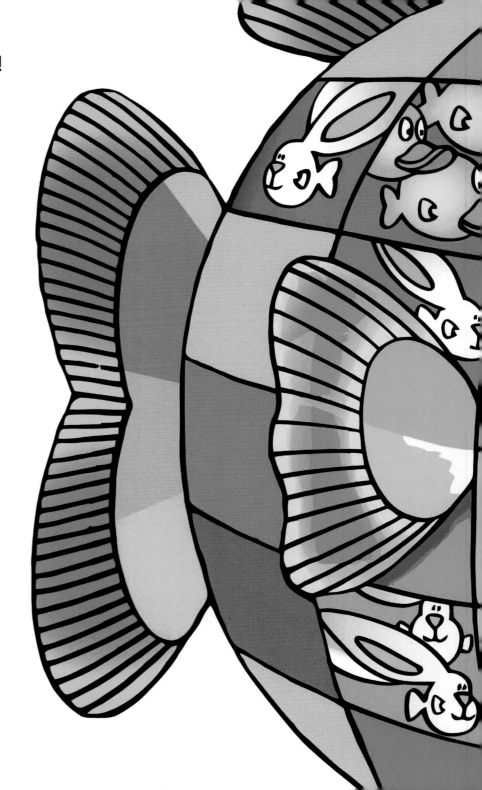

He saw the chicken fish, the flute fish, the hippo fish, and the tiger fish, too. And can you believe it? He swallowed them all up in one huge gulp.

He was making a pig fish out of himself.

I'm pretty full, he thought. But there's still one more fish left to swallow.

The fat cat fish!
Go for it, he thought to himself.
And go for it he did!

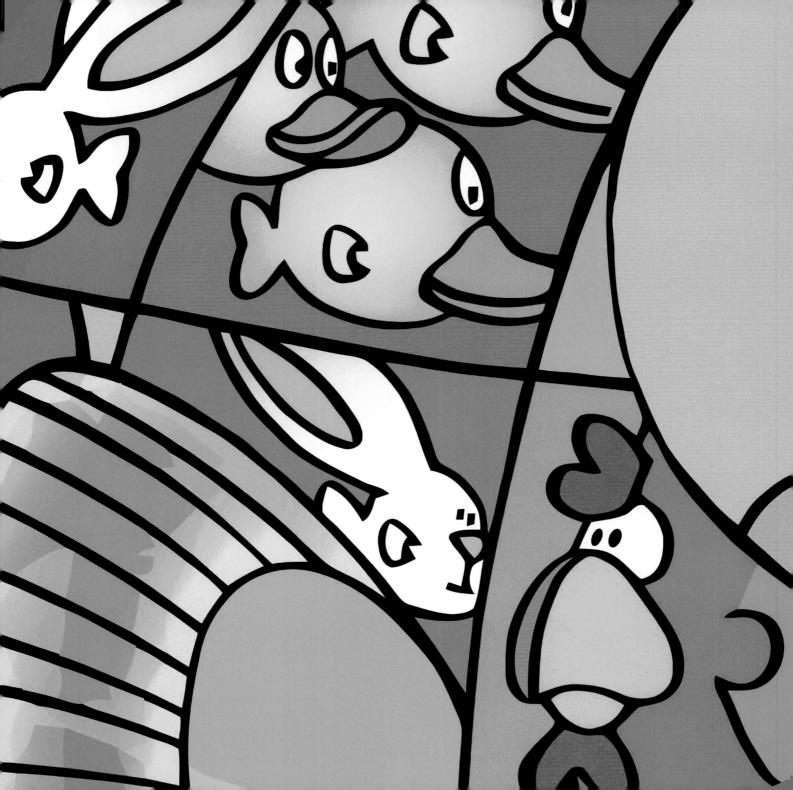

Now he was
so big
that he
took up the
whole
aquarium!

That was really good,
he thought. To top it off,
I think I'll have dessert now.
So he slurped down
some nice, slimy,
green plants.

That was a bad idea. He was feeling very, very full.

All of a sudden, the patchwork tooth fish burped.
What a huge, loud burp it was!
There were bubbles everywhere.

When the bubbles finally cleared, the patchwork tooth fish was back to his smaller, plain self...

...and the aquarium was filled with fish again.

There is no moral to this story, but if there was one, it would be "Don't bite off more than you can chew!"

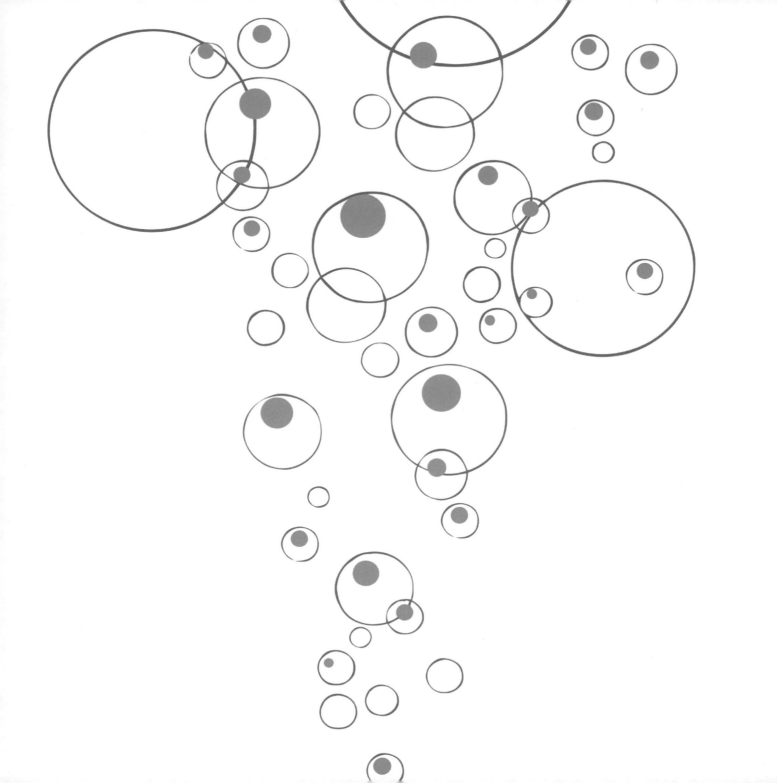

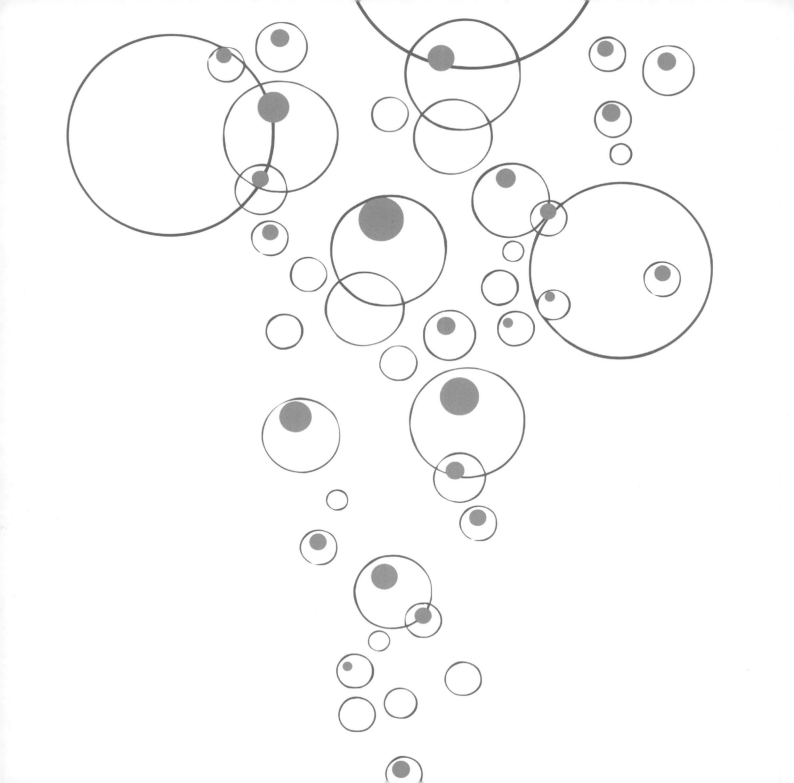

Made in the USA
Lexington, KY
05 September 2017